The Story of SMALL FRY

CONTENTS

THE STORY OF

*It was the morning after the
big storm...*

Mrs. Bixby walked along the
beach, looking for treasures that
the tide had carried in.
Suddenly, she saw something
strange in the water. "Is that
an old boot?" she said. Kicking
off her shoes, she waded into
the water. "My, oh my! An
injured seal pup!" she said in
surprise. "You must have gotten
lost in the storm. Maybe your
mother is looking for you."

MALL FRY

All afternoon, Mrs. Bixby
watched the seal pup from a
distance but there was no sign
of its mother. "You'd better
come home with me," she said
to the little seal pup. "I'll take
care of you the best I can."

Mrs. Bixby carried the seal pup home and put it in her pool. Then she called the seal rescue center on the mainland. Carefully, she wrote down all the instructions that the center gave her. She then made a special formula for the seal pup to drink, and she gently washed its wounds.

Formula
for Orphan
Seal Pup

Throughout the night, Mrs. Bixby fed the little orphan pup every few hours. "I shall have to call you Small Fry, because you are so small," she said. "If you can just make it through the night, I think you will be all right."

In the morning, Mrs. Bixby jumped out of bed and hurried to the pool. The little seal pup was sitting up in the water, looking alert.

"Boo-ma," it barked.

Mrs. Bixby laughed with relief. "That's a very big noise from such a small fry!" she said.

Day after day, the baby seal grew stronger. Its wounds healed, and it began to follow Mrs. Bixby around the island, like a puppy. Mrs. Bixby took the pup to the rock pools on the shore. She taught it how to catch fish. "You are the best treasure the tide ever brought to me," she said.

All summer long, Small Fry and Mrs. Bixby swam in the sea and sat on the beach at sunset. They became the best of friends.

One day, Mrs. Bixby took Small Fry swimming out beyond the surf line. Suddenly, a group of seals joined them. They splashed and barked and swam in circles around Small Fry. Small Fry watched them and barked. "Go, Small Fry!" said Mrs. Bixby. "Your family has found you at last."

Small Fry blinked at Mrs. Bixby, swam out to sea with the seals, and disappeared beyond the waves.

Mrs. Bixby swam back to
the shore and put on her
shoes. Slowly she walked
homeward along the beach.
She felt sad, but happy, too.

Suddenly, she saw something
strange in the water. "Is that
a feather duster?" she said.
Kicking off her shoes, she
waded into the water. "My, oh
my! An injured seagull!" she
said in surprise. "You'd better
come home with me!"

SEAL PUPS

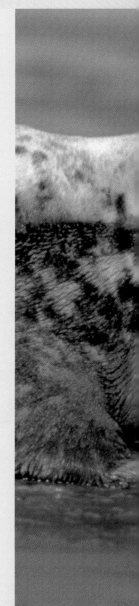

In the spring and early summer, large numbers of seals gather at rookeries to mate. Some rookeries have colonies of more than 100,000 seals.

Twelve months after mating, the females return to give birth, often at the same crowded rookery where they were born.

A female seal (or cow) usually gives birth to just one pup at a time. Even at a noisy, crowded rookery, a mother can recognize her pup by its cry and smell.

Sometimes, however, boats or people may frighten a mother seal away. A pup permanently separated from its mother is called an orphan. Without food and protection, an orphan seal pup will die. Many orphan seal pups are taken to rescue centers like the Wolf Hollow Center, where these photographs were taken. Here, orphans are cared for by skilled people.

Without food and protection from predators, this orphan seal pup was near death.

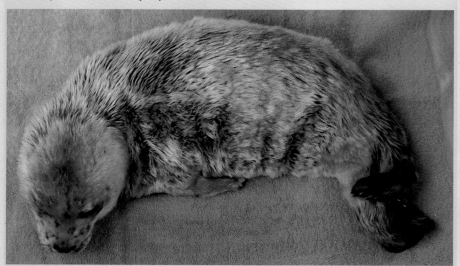

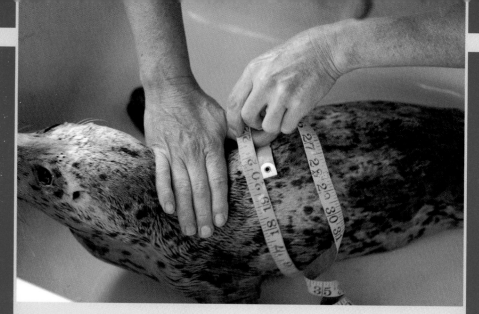

Upon their arrival at the rescue center, orphan pups are measured and weighed by the staff.

For the first few days, an orphan is kept in an individual bathtub and receives special attention.

Just like a human baby, a seal pup
needs special food. A formula made
from mashed fish, fish oil, vitamins, and
minerals is fed to the pup through a tube
that is gently pushed into its mouth.
When a pup is older, it will eat raw fish.

At first, a seal pup is fed through a tube.

When an orphan pup is older and stronger, it is introduced to a whole-fish diet by the staff.

Before long, young pups will chase the fish thrown into their pool by a caregiver.

By the time a seal pup is three months old, it can swim and catch live fish on its own. It has also acquired social skills that enable it to live with other seals. Soon, it will be transported in an animal carrier to a shallow bay near a known seal habitat. There, it will be released, ready to return to life in the sea.

Remember

Never pick up a seal pup! Sometimes a pup is just resting on the rocks or shore while its mother hunts for food. You can best help a lone pup by keeping an eye on it from a distance. If the mother has not returned to the pup after four hours, call the police or wildlife service for help.

Seal Lullaby

(Excerpt)

Where billow meets billow,
there soft be thy pillow;
ah, weary wee flipperling,
curl at thy ease!
The storm shall not wake thee,
nor sharks overtake thee,
asleep in the arms
of the slow-swinging sea.

– Rudyard Kipling

About the Author

Marcia Vaughan lives on Vashon Island in Puget Sound, near Seattle, Washington. She has always loved writing and, even as a preschooler, she enjoyed sitting on the back porch of her childhood home, telling her friends wild stories. *The Story of Small Fry* was inspired by observations of the harbor seals in Puget Sound.

The author wishes to thank Brian Joseph, Curator and Chief Veterinarian at the Point Defiance Zoo and Aquarium in Tacoma, Washington, and the kind people at the Wolf Hollow Rehabilitation Center at Friday Harbor, Washington, for their generous help.

Written by **Marcia Vaughan**
Illustrated by **John Hurford**
Edited by **Sue Ledington**
Designed by **Kristie Rogers**

Photography by **Hedgehog House:** Mark Hamblin (p.23); **Wolf Hollow Rehabilitation Center:** (pp. 24-29)

04 03 02 01 00
10 9 8 7 6 5 4

Distributed in the United States of America by
    Rigby
    a division of Reed Elsevier Inc.
    P.O. Box 797
    Crystal Lake, IL 60039-0797

Printed by Colorcraft, Hong Kong
ISBN: 0-7901-1672-3